T0381040

Tommy the Tooter Turtle

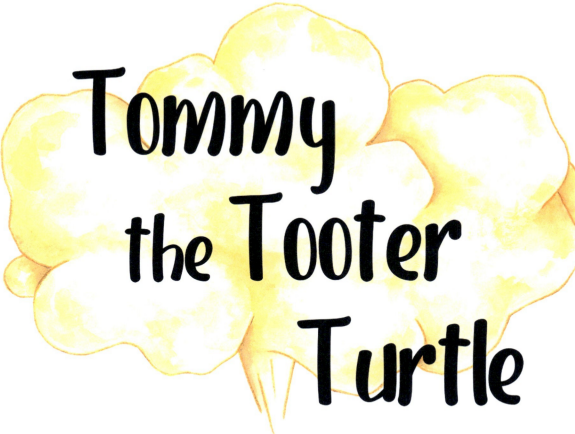

Written by Curt Munson

Illustrated by Courtney Kinter

AuthorHouse™
1663 Liberty Drive
Bloomington, IN 47403
www.authorhouse.com
Phone: 833-262-8899

Interior Image Credit: Courtney Kinter

This book is printed on acid-free paper.

ISBN: 978-1-6655-1219-0 (sc)
ISBN: 978-1-6655-1220-6 (e)

Print information available on the last page.

Published by AuthorHouse 02/10/2021

authorHOUSE®

Tommy Turtle lives in a beautiful little town named Mayfield. Well, not the whole town, after all he is a turtle and doesn't take up much space. In Mayfield there is a beautiful little park. In that beautiful little park is the County Courthouse, trees, bushes, flowers, grass and a beautiful little pond.

That is where Tommy Turtle lives, a beautiful little pond in a beautiful little park in a beautiful little town. Wouldn't it be fun if Tommy was beautiful too? Well, maybe to his mother he is beautiful, but to everyone else, Tommy is just a turtle. Even if Tommy is not beautiful, he may still be the very nicest box turtle you would ever want to meet.

Tommy doesn't live in the pond by himself. He lives there with all of his family and friends. Turtles don't move around much and Tommy has lived in the pond since the day he was hatched, he knows all of the other Turtles, and they all know him, which is a nice way to live. The turtles who live in the pond have a pretty good life. They like to swim, they like to eat, and they love to sleep. Tommy does all of those things. In fact, in almost every way, Tommy is just like the other turtles in the pond.

But NOT in every way.

You see, Tommy Turtle has a secret. It is a secret because he doesn't want to talk about it. He doesn't want to talk about it because it is embarrassing. It is embarrassing because, well there is just no nice way to say it: Tommy is a tooter. That's right, a tooter. Don't act like you don't know what toot means. It means the same in turtle that it does in human. He toots. A lot.

Tommy wasn't always a tooter. Once upon a time, he was just like the other turtles. You know, just an occasional toot. Every turtle toots occasionally, even though the girl turtles like to deny it. But Tommy isn't like every turtle, Tommy is a tooter and when he toots, he really TOOTS

Every year, the Mayfield turtles hold the Turtle Olympics. There are events in digging, walking (turtles don't run) and of course swimming. In the swimming finals, Tommy was racing against Emmy Didae, the fastest swimmer in the whole pond. Tommy didn't think he would win because Emmy never lost a swimming race. Just before the race began, Tommy's best friend, Marina Testudo said to him, "Just do your best Tommy, that is all you can do.

Finally the time for the race arrived. Turtles
don't have starter pistols so Grandpa
Leatherback just said, "You can swim on the
surface or under the water. Just get to the
finish line first and you win. On your mark, get
set, GO," and the race began! Right away,
Emmy sped ahead and soon Tommy could
barely see her. Thinking he would lose made
Tommy nervous, and being nervous gives him
gas. Suddenly, Tommy felt a toot coming on, so
he dived under the water to prevent the turtles
watching the race from hearing him.

Tommy didn't just toot, he tooted like ten turtles, and the gas propelled him all the way across the pond like he was riding an underwater rocket. Tommy went under Emmy like she was swimming in a circle, and to the amazement of everyone watching, Tommy surfaced at the finish line long before Emmy got there swimming on the surface.

Tommy won the race! Tommy never told anyone how he won, because there are some things nice turtles just don't talk about.

Although it is a small town, Mayfield is the county seat and that is why Mayfield has a courthouse. Because there are no other towns nearby, Mayfield also has lots of churches, schools, stores, offices and even some very nice banks. Because it is such a small town, all of the churches, stores, schools, offices and banks were built near the courthouse.

This was very good news for Tommy, because in all of those churches, schools, stores, offices and banks there were people who like to walk in the park during their breaks from work or school. Tommy loves to see the humans come to the park and walk around the pond. He really likes people. Liking people is another thing that makes Tommy very different from the other turtles. All of the other turtles are afraid of people.

Tommy and his friends like to climb up on the rocks around the pond and bask in the sunshine on nice days. Unlike Tommy, whenever a person would walk nearby, all of the other turtles would slide off of their rocks and hide in the water until the people went on by.

Tommy loved to see the people. He thought they were ever so funny looking. He would always get onto his feet and stretch his neck out of his shell to look at the humans when they were nearby. He stretched his neck so far that his mouth would open and some people even thought he was smiling at them. If Tommy ever knew what a smile was he would almost certainly have tried to have one for the people who walked by, because he liked them a lot.

One of the stores near the park is a pet store, and the owners of the pet store sell little bags of pellets that are safe for the turtles to eat. Almost every day people buy those little bags of turtle food pellets and come to the park and throw the pellets into the water for the turtles to eat. Those pellets are one of the reasons Tommy likes the people so much. When they throw food to him, Tommy doesn't have to spend time looking for food for that day. That means he has time to do other things. There are lots of things he likes to do much more than hunt for food.

Tommy and his friend Marina Testudo like to swim. They also like to dive to the bottom of the pond. Turtles can stay under water a very long time. Sometimes turtles even sleep on the bottom of the pond without running out of air. Marina likes to dive to the bottom every time a person walks by.

Tommy only likes to dive when all of the humans are at work or in school, and of course, sometimes he dives to the bottom just before he toots so his friends won't hear or smell him.

One day Tommy found a new plant growing on the edge of the pond. He called Marina to come and look at it with him. Marina called her father and mother to come look at the new plant and they called their mother and father to come and look and pretty soon all of the turtles were looking at the new plant growing at the corner of the pond.

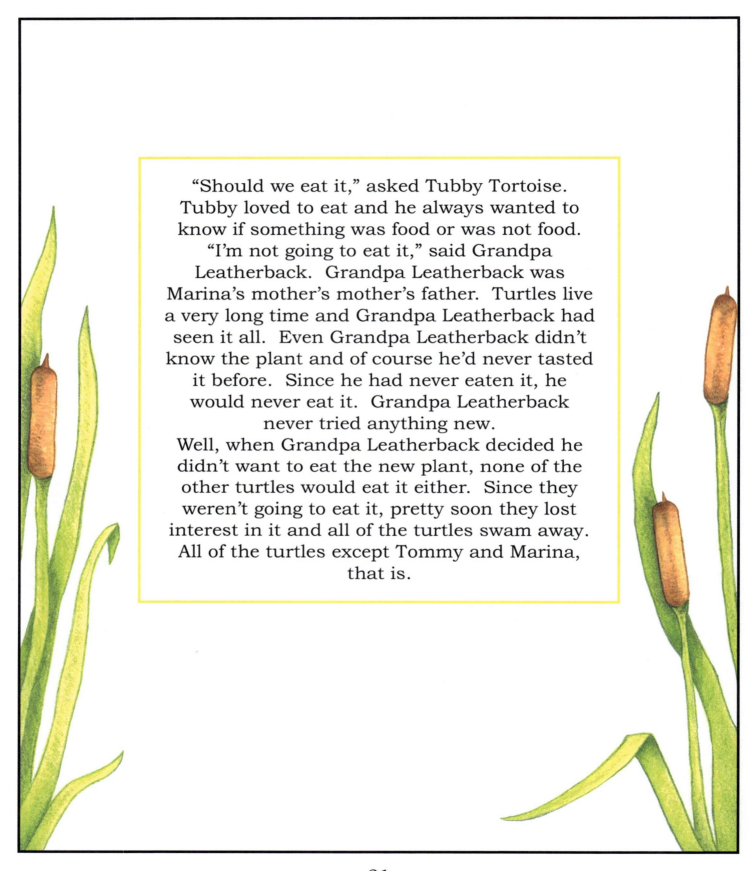

"Should we eat it," asked Tubby Tortoise. Tubby loved to eat and he always wanted to know if something was food or was not food.

"I'm not going to eat it," said Grandpa Leatherback. Grandpa Leatherback was Marina's mother's mother's father. Turtles live a very long time and Grandpa Leatherback had seen it all. Even Grandpa Leatherback didn't know the plant and of course he'd never tasted it before. Since he had never eaten it, he would never eat it. Grandpa Leatherback never tried anything new.

Well, when Grandpa Leatherback decided he didn't want to eat the new plant, none of the other turtles would eat it either. Since they weren't going to eat it, pretty soon they lost interest in it and all of the turtles swam away. All of the turtles except Tommy and Marina, that is.

"I think we ought to eat it," Tommy told Marina after the other turtles had swum away from the new plant.

"But what if it is dangerous?" Marina asked.

"Well," Tommy replied, "in that case, we shouldn't eat very much until we know if it will make us sick."

"What do you mean us?" Marina said, very surprised.

"You and me," Tommy answered. "You're my best friend. I want to share it with you."

"But I don't want to share it with you!" Marina informed him. "Grandpa Leatherback doesn't want to eat it and if is not good enough for my mother's mother's father, well, then it's not good enough for me."

"But Marina, if we can eat it, then we won't have to hunt for food today and we can do other things."

"But Tommy, hunting for food is what Turtles do when we are not sunning ourselves or sleeping on the bottom of the pond."

"Oh pooh," Tommy said.

"Oh pooh yourself," Marina said right back. Marina then swam away to join the other turtles on the other side of the pond.

Tommy sat and looked at the plant. His stomach was rumbling and he knew he was going to have to eat the plant or start hunting for something else to have for lunch.

"I'm going to eat it," Tommy said.

He climbed up on the bank and began to eat the plant.

"Oh look," a nearby human said, "that turtle is eating a broccoli plant. I didn't know turtles ate broccoli. I hope it doesn't give him gas."

Of course Tommy doesn't speak human so he didn't know what the people were saying. He just kept eating the plant until his tummy was full.

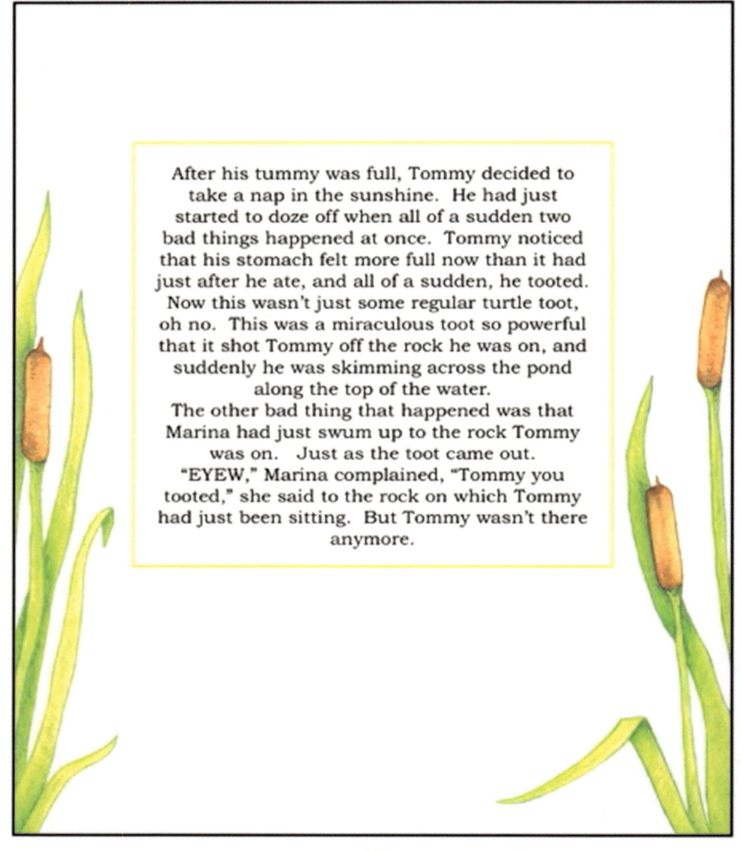

After his tummy was full, Tommy decided to take a nap in the sunshine. He had just started to doze off when all of a sudden two bad things happened at once. Tommy noticed that his stomach felt more full now than it had just after he ate, and all of a sudden, he tooted. Now this wasn't just some regular turtle toot, oh no. This was a miraculous toot so powerful that it shot Tommy off the rock he was on, and suddenly he was skimming across the pond along the top of the water.

The other bad thing that happened was that Marina had just swum up to the rock Tommy was on. Just as the toot came out.

"EYEW," Marina complained, "Tommy you tooted," she said to the rock on which Tommy had just been sitting. But Tommy wasn't there anymore.

She turned just in time to see Tommy skimming along the top of the water in the pond at about 50 miles an hour. Well, I don't know how much you know about turtles, but a turtle who can go across a pond at 50 miles per hour is just never seen.

"WOW!" Tommy called out to Marina as he was swimming back to the bank. "That was AWESOME!"
"Weren't you scared?" Marina asked.
"Not really," Tommy answered, "except that I almost lifted up from the water. I had to drag all four of my legs in the water to keep from flying out of the pond."

"Well don't do that again," Marina ordered him.
"Marina," Tommy said.
"What?" Marina replied.
"I'm going to toot again!" And no sooner had he said it, than he did it!

BRAAAPPPPP. And Tommy was off again, skimming across the top of the water. This time he was on his back and couldn't drag his legs in the water to slow himself down, and guess what? HE FLEW!

Now Tommy didn't fly very much, he only went a couple of feet out of the water before he crashed back in, but boy did he ever love it.

This time it took a long time for Tommy to swim back to Marina, but when he got close he called out, "Marina, did you see me? I flew!"

"Not only did I see you," Marina complained, "I smelled you, too!"

"I'm sorry about that, Marina, but that was really fun. I got a little scared and pulled my legs into my shell, but if they had been out, I think I could have turned and flown right back here."

"Tommy, don't do that any more. I'm afraid you could get hurt, or even worse."

"It's too late, Marina, I'm getting ready to do it again!"

BRAAAPPP. And Tommy flew off across the pond again. This time though, he wasn't afraid. He got up to speed and pulled his head straight up and flew up into the sky. Tommy then put his arms out of the shell and by putting them down or up, learned how to turn. He actually got turned completely around and flew back towards Marina.

On his way back to the other side of the pond,
Tommy flew over Grandpa Leatherback and the
other turtles.
"LOOK AT ME!" Tommy called to them "I'M
FLYING!"
"Well, I never," Grandpa Leatherback said, "I never
flew before, and I never saw any other turtles fly
either."

"Marina," Tommy cried out jubilantly after he made a kind of crazy splashing landing near his friend.. "I not only flew, I could control it. That was the greatest thing that ever happened to me. I'm a flyer!!!"

"But Tommy," Marina complained, "you're also a tooter, you're Tommy the Tooter Turtle."

Printed in the United States
By Bookmasters